For my Nanu, Dadu, fufus, chachis, mamis, and khalas,
and all the remarkable women I am blessed to call family.
Most of all, for the four chambers of my heart, Maa, Boo, Asiya, and Amina.
—R. C.

To my mother, who carries stories of strength,
courage, and hope in every fold of her sari.
—L. N.

the Katha Chest

Radhiah Chowdhury

illustrated by

Lavanya Naidu

SALAAM
READS

NEW YORK | LONDON | TORONTO
SYDNEY | NEW DELHI

Asiya loves going to Nanu's house.

It is filled with all sorts of treasures.
And the best treasure of all is the katha chest.

For years, Nanu made katha quilts out of all the old saris Maa and her sisters didn't wear anymore, and all the kathas are hidden in that chest.

Asiya likes to crawl inside and burrow into the soft, warm quilts. She imagines them whispering soft, warm stories to her.

She traces the golden threads on a blue and purple quilt.
The circular patterns look like the old medal that
Boro Khala sometimes lets her play with.

Boro Khala says the medal comes from a sad time
when Boro Khalu was away. . . .

Asiya trip-traps her fingers over the splodges
of paint on a bright yellow quilt.

They remind her of the way Mejo Khala's fingers are always stained with bright colors.

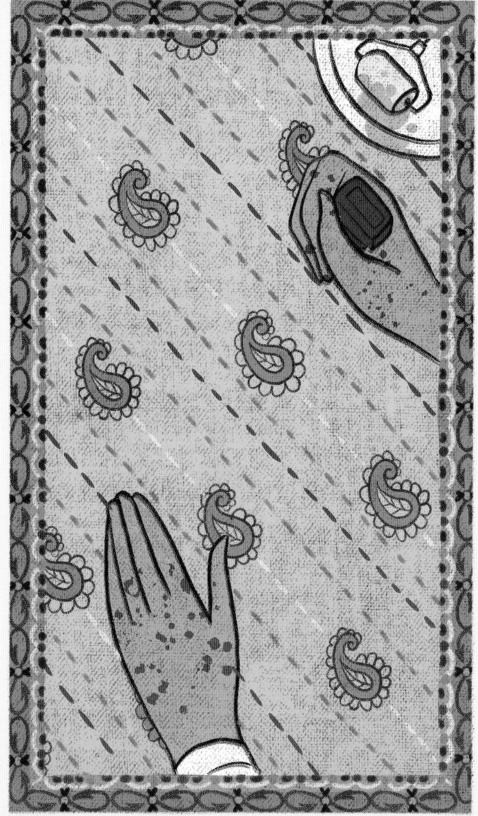

One of the quilts is folded with neat, stiff edges.

When Shejo Khala laughs and spins Asiya around in a circle, her clothes still have neat, stiff edges. She's never messy.

A thick white streak runs across another quilt, like
the white saris Choto Khala has worn since Khalu died.

Asiya imagines it is the road to the village
where Choto Khala still lives.

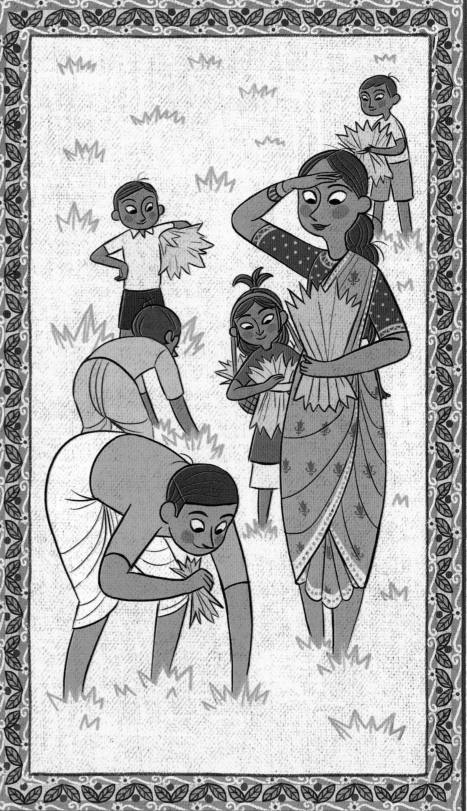

Asiya's favorite quilt is the patchworked one that
looks the most different from the others, with strange
two-legged shapes making strange two-legged patterns.

She knows it is Maa's because it smells like ink and
tomato sauce and home.

Maa and the Khalas take the quilts out of the katha chest when everyone comes together to drink tea, tell stories, and remember Nanu.

When everyone else is gone and the house is quiet,
Maa wraps Asiya tightly in the quilt that is
paper-thin with age, and smells like tea and
old books and porcelain and wood.

And she tells Asiya the story of Nanu's quilt,
the oldest quilt of all.

Author's Note

In Bangladesh, where my mother grew up, kathas are light quilts used in every household. The art of making a katha is a special skill. Fashioned from layers of cotton saris so old as to have become unwearable, kathas tell their stories in the fabric itself, the stories of the everyday lives of the women who wore those saris and then painstakingly stitched them together to give comfort to their households.

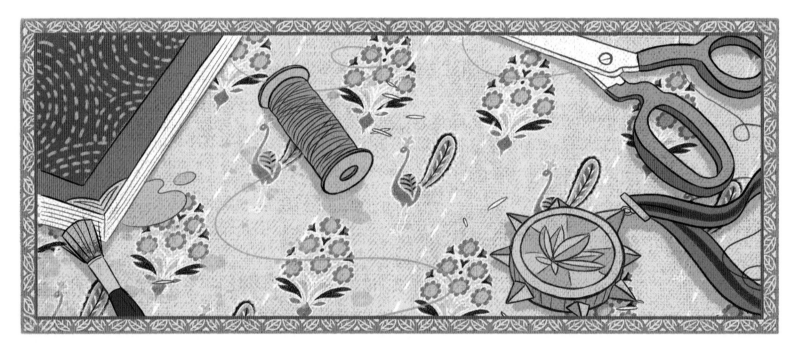

Illustrator's Note

When I was growing up in Kolkata, my mother's cupboard of saris was always under lock and key. On the occasions that this cupboard was opened, my excitement knew no bounds! A hundred stories all wrapped within the pleats of these gorgeous textiles lay before me. *The Katha Chest* resonated with me for the same reasons. Each pattern created for the aunts' quilts is inspired by Radhiah's family saris as well as my own. The past spreads are inspired by the Bengali folk art called Pattachitra—cloth paintings with simple colors, bold lines, and intricate details.

SALAAM
READS

An imprint of Simon & Schuster Children's Publishing Division

1230 Avenue of the Americas, New York, New York 10020

Text © 2021 by Radhiah Chowdhury

Illustration © 2021 by Lavanya Naidu

Book design © 2022 by Simon & Schuster, Inc.

Originally published in 2021 in Australia by Allen & Unwin

First US edition 2022

For information about special discounts for bulk purchases, please contact Simon & Schuster

Special Sales at 1-866-506-1949 or business@simonandschuster.com.

The Simon & Schuster Speakers Bureau can bring authors to your live event. For more information or to book an event,

contact the Simon & Schuster Speakers Bureau at 1-866-248-3049 or visit our website at www.simonspeakers.com.

The text for this book was set in Century Gothic Std.

Manufactured in China

1121 SCP

2 4 6 8 10 9 7 5 3 1

Library of Congress Cataloging-in-Publication Data

Names: Chowdhury, Radhiah, author. | Naidu, Lavanya, illustrator.

Title: The katha chest / Radhiah Chowdhury ; illustrated by Lavanya Naidu.

Description: First edition. | New York : Salaam Reads / Simon & Schuster Books for Young Readers, [2022] |

Audience: Ages 4 to 8. | Audience: Grades K-1.

| Summary: Asiya loves to visit Nanu's house and rummage through her kath chest filled

with quilts that tell stories about the bold and brave women in Asiya's family.

Identifiers: LCCN 2021016209 (print) | LCCN 2021016210 (ebook) | ISBN 9781665903905 (hardcover) | ISBN 9781665903912 (ebook)

Subjects: CYAC: Quilts—Fiction. | Grandmothers—Fiction. | Mothers—Fiction. | Aunts—Fiction. | LCGFT: Picture books.

Classification: LCC PZ7.1.C5427 Kat 2022 (print) | LCC PZ7.1.C5427 (ebook) | DDC [E]—dc23

LC record available at https://lccn.loc.gov/2021016209

LC ebook record available at https://lccn.loc.gov/2021016210